"An admirable first effort by a very young author who has chosen to dive into the grim noir world of the 1950's portrayed in the black and white films of the genre. A young and vulnerable girl runs away to New York encountering many of the city's perils. Criminals abound and dramatic troubles ensue, but in the end, she finds her inner strength to extricate herself from a dangerous relationship. The story foretells a bright future for this young writer."

– Philip and Judith Frick

"In her first novella, Dree Christiano treats her readers to a moving tale of God's redemption and grace. She skillfully develops her characters and weaves them into an unforgettable storyline."

– Kandy Ellis

Carmen...

A Story of Inconceivable Grace

Dree Christiano

Illustrations by Teryn Pepper

Cover Design by Dree Christiano

For questions and comments, contact at:

books.by.dree@gmail.com

Or on Instagram at:

@books.by.dree

*If this story holds any resemblance to any persons, living or dead, the case is purely coincidental.

Published by Books by Dree

ISBN-13:978-0-9963474-1-9

For God's precious children,
who deserve second chances.

For those who think there is nothing else.
Hold on, reach out to God.
He will set you on your feet again,
and walk with you. I promise you that the
storm will pass. I've been there,
and now I've written this book for you.

Psalm 147:3 says:
"He heals the brokenhearted,
and binds up their wounds."

Preface

Preface

Once... there was a girl, Carmen Everett. From early in her youth she was despised for her beauty and turned heads. For many of her days she hated where she was brought up, and how she was brought up. In a small farm community, in the middle of nowhere, under her father's demanding, controlling roof.

"I'm helping you, Carrie." he used to say. *"When you get out on your own, you'll be glad you've been brought up with morals and structure."*

To little teenage Carrie, structure was not fun and was not enough to keep her at home. Fifteen, then sixteen, then seventeen. She warned her father that when she turned eighteen, she was leaving. He never believed her. He laughed at her.

"You won't leave." he'd threaten. *"How will you get along? How will you live? You don't know how to do anything. You're worth nothing."*

He was wrong, they were all wrong. She knew how to make friends, didn't she? She had looks, didn't she? You can ride a long way on that ticket in a big city.

So off she went. New York, and Grand Central Station. A subway to Brooklyn.

Wanted: Girl with a good voice to sing. Apply, The Hot Spot. 1515 Kenston St.

January 1952,
Brooklyn, New York

It's the same old story. Just another dingy night in the city; just another gun moll. Steam escaping from subway grates. In a city that never sleeps, there is a typical nocturnal scene...

Chapter 1

The mood. It's always about the mood, with this sort of thing. You know...the horn blowing across the street; tonight, it plays the especially haunting refrain of "Angel Eyes". The rain beating down into the streets below. A man in a raincoat, scurrying to find shelter. The slam of a car door, and then the bumping and giggling of a guy and his gal out of a taxi. Cats screaming in the alley. The smoky, dim-lit room.

The ashtray overflowing, and a glass clinking as the woman pours another out of the half a bottle of wine she's drained all by herself.

Everybody knows what she looks like. A peach of a bottle blonde, with blood-red lips, and matching nails. You can see her now, can't you? No, don't lie, you know you do. She's cute, isn't she? And, oh, those eyes. And she's tall, she's very tall, about five-feet-six, don't you think?

She's the kind that every woman wishes to be, and every man wants to own.

Her eyes are sad and framed with moisture. Her lip quivers, hiding her sobs. Oh boy, you're really feeling sorry for her now, you poor sap. And then the pacing. She looks up at the clock, and then out the window again. Her pace slows, slightly. She flops on her bed, dejected, but relieved that she can finally sleep. But she jerks up to a groaning, and loud slamming of the door. Her hair stands on end at the scene that will be played out next…

"Carmen!" he growls, stumbling into the flat.

Her heart beats at the seeming speed of a hummingbird's wings. He strides over to her with that threatening way of his. It is useless to ask where he's been; for she knows.

Shoving her back into the bedroom, he kicks the door shut. He grabs her hair and pins her to the wall. "Have you been a good girl while I was away?" he hisses, kissing her jaw.

His kisses made her want to melt in his arms, and why? What kind of loving was his?

"Toni stop, please stop." she pushes him away. That was her big mistake. He hits her across the face, making it numb, and then sting.

How has she forgotten? She must never resist Toni. Her mind was so fuzzy, so tired, all reason fled her.

Carmen was sore at Toni for what he did to her the last two nights, plus coming home plastered. But she still managed to get up and fix him breakfast, wondering all the while why she was doing it. She only knew how to fry eggs, toast bread on a skillet, and make pancakes (which had become staples), but Toni didn't usually complain.

"Toni! Get up!" she hollered, heaping a fried egg on Tina's plate. "Good heavens, it's freezing in here!"

Carmen rubbed her shoulders, the thin red satin robe did nothing to warm her. The Brooklyn snow was deep and slushy, and the cheap flat was as good as sleeping outside.

"Keep your voice down, will ya?" Toni groaned, holding his head, and fumbled to a sitting position.

Carmen's heart pounded like a wild animal inside a cage - he wasn't going to be in a good mood today. But her groaning heart was silenced by her groaning stomach that had not received food in two mornings. The breakfast was silent, as most times had become between Carmen and Toni.

"Can I go out and play, Aunt Carmen?" Tina asked, scooping a large bite of pancake into her mouth.

"Ask your mother after breakfast," Toni answered, holding up his newspaper to the dim light filtering through the window.

Carmen often felt sorry for the little girl who was not like most little girls. She did not have many friends, and the ones she had she treasured. She was rather small, and the older and bigger kids picked on her. She hadn't many toys, and she lived in a cold, filthy apartment. She was not allowed to play for long, nor to speak to adults - and forbidden to talk about her family to anyone and everyone.

Chapter 2

Carmen stared at her drooping, darkened eyes. *How'd I get here?* She frequently found herself asking. The question only furthered to bewilder her.

Here she was in New York.

Her mind drifted to thoughts of her Kansas hometown, and family. She'd been so young and stupid when she decided the prairie flowers and dust were not enough for her adventurous spirit. On the brink of turning eighteen, and finishing high school, she ran away. She gathered every penny she had ever saved and pawned jewelry of hers to get enough money for the fares, and a room. She had reached New York and started a job as a nightclub singer. She had met Toni at her job. She was hot and sassy then. Ted, her boss, had begun his growth on Carmen's heart before Toni had. But she and Toni had eventually grown closer, and she moved in with him, Maria, Alessandro, and newborn Tina. She should have known then that he was trouble.

Her attention snapped back to the present, listening to Toni in a hushed voice on the telephone with a man. Her blood turned cold. She finished her makeup and brushed out her curls in a tasseled, free look. She had learned the style that her fans at The Hot Spot preferred. She struggled with applying her false eyelashes, as was so common for her. She exited the bedroom, and Toni looked her up and down, giving her a silent whistle of praise. His look made her uneasy. She knew what he thought of her job. His jealous tendencies could make him very hostile. The result was it being taken out on her. She sucked in a breath, and nervously got her things together.

"I gotta go." Toni quickly hung up the phone. He noticed her stiffen as he lit a cigarette. He could tell she knew that the phone call wasn't just a pleasant, *"how do you do?"*.

Carmen ran to him. "Toni, what was that phone call about? Who was that man?"

Toni placed his hands on her arms firmly. "Nothing that you need to worry that beautiful face about."

"Please, Toni. I've got to know."

"No such thing." Toni snapped. He softened for a moment and kissed her.

"It's getting late. I have to go." She started for the door, and then paused. "I love you, Toni." She ran back and threw her arms around his neck for one final embrace. He responded in a cooler, unemotional manner with a squeeze around her waist and peck.

Once in the doorway, she looked back. "Do you love me, Toni?"

"You know I do, baby." He winked. Carmen knew he was lying, but shrugged, and stepped into the hallway, and started her trek down the five flights of stairs.

The jazz band leaped into the snappy tune of *"Why Don't You Do Right?"*.

The warm spotlight hit Carmen. Her long, strapless, black-sequined gown shimmered under the brightness. Her red silk gloves glowed. Her dangling diamond earrings swung back and forth with every move she made. Her leg peeped out from the thigh-high slit in her gown. She was spectacular! All eyes were on her. All the eyes were male, of course. She did a few sharp hip swings, quick jabs of her knee, and then wandered down to where the guys were sitting. She whipped her head back and forth, her platinum blonde hair flying. Maneuvering around the tables, she seduced every one of them.

Ted stepped out of his office to mingle with his guests, and to enjoy a lingering look at his star that brought in the business. He was her haven from the pit she lived in, and the man she lived with. She just couldn't get it right with her men. He may be safe, but he also had a ring on his finger.

Ted felt sorry for her when she'd come to him out of need as a young girl, looking for a job. She had lived out of her dressing room for several months, before catching Toni's eye.

Toni had been a friend of his, for quite a long time. He'd seen Toni around plenty, Toni only staying around long enough to get someone hooked on whatever mysterious drug he possessed.

He still recalled the night that Toni took half of her away from him. Not that he was selfishly jealous of Toni, but he hated to see a selfless, beautiful woman like Carmen be thrown to a hungry wolf.

He knew that he was going to lose her.

Carmen was finishing her spot. The men that surrounded her whooped and hollered at her performance; she tried her best to make it worth their while. The look, deep in her eyes revealed that she didn't get a kick out of performing in front of a bunch of men. Ted felt horrible, throwing a diamond into a dump.

And then Toni walks in. Ted could feel the tension rising, though all eyes and ears were on Carmen, with her attractive figure, and soothing voice. Toni took a seat, and seemed to fit in with the rest of the crowd. Carmen was immediately lured to him.

"Carmen, you cannot possibly be serious about all of this!" Ted searched for her eyes that were fixed to the wall. "You're eighteen, Carmen. You have no idea how to handle much of anything yet; you're still just a kid. You have no idea how I feel about this."

Carmen crossed her arms. "You seem to forget, Ted darling, that I'm the one having an affair with a thirty-year-old married man." She shot back, her tone dripping with sarcasm.

"I never forced you into any of this!" he voiced that comment louder than he had intended.

"All I'm saying is that I need to think of myself here. I can't go on like this forever since I'm only the 'other woman'. I need to start thinking of my future, what I want. If you really love me, Ted, you'll let me live as I see fit."

All Ted could see was a child throwing a temper tantrum, not a woman speaking reason.

"Okay, Carmen. I do love you, I want you to know. I want you to do what you please, and be happy. When you need me, I'll be here." He kissed her forehead. "I just want you to know that he's not what he seems. He is dangerous."

In Carmen's mind, she was simply living in the moment. Going all out before her body succumbed to age. Young women often find dangerous to be exciting, that of which, Ted lacked. Toni was attractive, and slightly gruff, and not sweet. The gruffness could be overlooked, even adored. Of course, she could never explain her motives to Ted. They would all seem so incredibly ridiculous to him.

"I will be careful. I love you, Ted. I will always love you." She pulled him close.

Ted had that reassurance. She had come to him frequently in the weeks of beginning her relationship with Toni.

She went along with Toni. With everything. Each time she came back to work, a little more of her was eaten away…

And now Ted stared at her from behind the wet bar, the only female in the smoke-filled place, and none could easily take their eyes off her. She sneaked a wink at him.

~

After three more songs, Carmen headed toward the wet bar to Ted. Five men, who were regulars, followed her and were in competition for who would occupy the seats on either side of her.

"Okay, what'll ya have, boys?" she looked left and right.

"Scotch."

"Rye."

"Bourbon."

"Margarita for me, honey." she smiled at Ted.

For the duration of the evening, she put up with the hoots, hollers, and catcalls, and was glad when she was finally allowed to go home. Ted waved a finger at her to come and get her pay.

"Baby, you were really great tonight." he placed the money in her hand and sneaked an arm around her waist.

"There's a little extra for you."

Too bad the money wasn't to stay in her nylons for long.

For a long moment, Carmen felt eyes on her, but when she turned, she saw no one.

"Thanks, honey." she kissed him.

~

Toni had just witnessed Carmen's hand in Ted's and was fuming. He stepped into the shadows and waited. He was there to make sure that she came home with him, and not with one of her clients, or her boss; he knew it had happened before. He was the jealous type. But Carmen was a beautiful woman. A bomb one had to be careful with, lest it go off in the wrong place, at the wrong time.

~

Carmen took the extra money, (a hundred bucks tonight), took up the rug, and pulled up a plank of wood from the floor. She took out the metal box. She carefully placed the money in the box and put it back with as much ease as she had taken it out. Nobody would ever know. She now had five hundred dollars. She then took her hat, gloves, and coat out of the closet. She positioned her fedora slightly over her eye and stuffed the wad of money in her right pocket.

As she left her dressing room, she was caught by a masculine grasp. She smiled before Ted wrapped her tightly into a kiss.

"Goodnight, honey." he smiled. She returned the same expression.

Carmen exited the club from the stage door into the alley. She caught her breath as a man's large frame towered over her and blocked her path.

"Toni." she breathed.
He flashed that sinister grin of his that always said: "Happy to see me, baby?" in his typical degrading manner.

"Toni, you-you startled me. I-I wasn't expecting to see you here."

"I just wanted to make sure my gal got home safe." He put a possessive arm around her waist and kissed her neck. She said nothing and let him lead her down the alley.

"D'ya get the dough?" he tapped her shoulder with his fist, holding a cigarette.

"Yes, Toni," she said curtly.

"So, how was it?" Toni edged.

"Usual. Fine, I guess." she shrugged.

"Did they get a good show?" he asked harshly, with an undertone of dry humor.

"I guess so." Carmen had the feeling he was trying to get at something.

"Was anyone else impressed?" Toni glanced at her.

"I'm sure I don't know what you mean."

"Stop playing games, Carmen. I know you're not just a singer at that guy's nightclub."

"What makes you think that?"

"You know I know that. And maybe you didn't see me, but I was outside the club tonight, during your cute, secret meeting." Toni stopped her, halfway down the second alley.

"Toni, it's none of your affair. But if you must know, Ted was handing me my pay."

"Let's just hope that's all it was, or I-" he stopped and flipped a mound of blonde, silky hair off her shoulders. His large hand gently closed around Carmen's neck, and his thumb pressed lightly on her voice box. It was almost large enough to fully encase it. Carmen froze in fear. And then the hand relaxed, and he bent down to kiss her. He had done that before. Why did he frighten her so?

"Come on, Toni." Carmen gently pushed him away. "I'm cold, and it's getting late."

Chapter 3

A week later, Carmen came leisurely out of the bedroom and yawned, stretching her arms to the sky. But she stopped short when she looked in front of her at Toni's tall, burly figure slumped in a chair. Then she knew she had to be in bright spirits.

"Good morning, Toni." Carmen put her arms around Toni's shoulders and gave his cheek a kiss.

"Morning, Carmen." he made no gesture of affection towards her but raked his hand through his hair.

"Could I get you something to eat?" Carmen went towards the stove and picked up the percolator sitting on the counter space.

"No."

Just 'no'? No 'thanks anyway'? No nothing. Sadness assailed her. What was she thinking? This was Toni, not Ted. Ted would have jerked up, said good morning, given her a kiss. He would have insisted that she sit while he got her coffee, and then she would have sat on his lap, talking the morning away. Disappointment kicked her heart, remembering that she wasn't with Ted this morning.

Sipping her black coffee in the kitchen, she still watched Toni. Her eyes were glued to him. She brought her robe closer around her neck.

"Carmen," Toni glanced at her, darkly. "Come 'ere, will ya."

Carmen carefully set her cup down and crept towards Toni like a cat, watching her each and every step. "What, Toni?"

"Carmen, where's the rest of that money?" Toni glared at her. "It's been short. I've counted it."

Carmen froze. She'd been putting back a little money - just a little - every night for the last few days. She'd thought she'd taken too little out that Toni could never notice, but apparently, she'd failed.

"Well, Toni- I-I wanted-needed-some new nylons - see I caught them on a bed spring when I crawled under the bed to get my shoes. And that's the other thing-those shoes, you know how I've been complaining about the padding coming out of the soles-I needed a new pair. That's what the money was for Toni. That's all. I promise." Carmen quickly lied. Her hands fumbled, and her gut twisted with guilt. She needed the money in case she finally got the nerve to leave him.

"I want to see them."

"I haven't found the right shade of nylons yet, and you know what a hard time I have with finding shoes." her voice was amazingly steady with that round of lies.

"I'm the one who decides where the money goes around here."

"And I'm the one who earns it!" Carmen raised her voice.

"Didn't I scrape you off the street when you were freezing to death?" Toni jumped from his chair, and flung it to the floor, it skittered almost a foot before it stopped. "Didn't I give you a roof over your head when you needed it most?" he shouted. Toni was in her face now, like a mad dog. The casual tiff about money had now become quite a heated argument.

"Toni, I'm the one paying for that roof! Not to mention most of the bills, and some of the groceries. I shouldn't have to answer to you if I need something."

"You're getting awfully lippy for a dame whose life depends on me." he lowered his voice, and slapped her, which to Carmen was scarier than his hollering.

"Besides, I don't trust you with money. You're gonna take off with that wolf of yours any day now to leave me in the dust." He took off, pushing her back against the wall, pinning her to it. Her hand was sealed to the wall, and Toni's hand was on her waist. Her face screwed up, anticipating what might come next. He took a large section of platinum hair in his hand and planted a kiss on her lips by force.

"Listen, and get this straight." Toni barked in her face again. "You're mine. And I'm not gonna let you run away with some hoodlum that'll drop you the second he finds someone else. But I just bet you're gonna run to him anyway." his breath touched her lips, and they quivered.

"Give me one good reason why I shouldn't." Carmen somehow got the strength to spew out from a bent neck. And then his hand scrunched her hair tighter. "Toni." she whimpered.

Toni's hand relaxed and stroked her silken, curly locks. "Carmen, you-you know I didn't mean that...I just, don't want to lose you is all. I love you, Carmen, you know that. I just want to protect you. You're so beautiful, I don't want anybody to snatch you away." he said it so softly, so gently, it made her want to forget everything he'd ever done to hurt her. The abused did tend to want to go back to their abusers. But she didn't realize she wanted him so.

"Darling, I'm sorry. Forgive me, please. I want you so." Toni pressed his cheek to hers and then kissed it.

"Of course, Toni." she breathed.

"And you're still my girl?"

"Yes, Toni." she nodded. *"Yes, Toni." "No, Toni."* over and over.

"Good." he smiled. "Tell you what, tomorrow we'll go shopping, and we can go to all the shops you want in search of the perfect pair of shoes, and the perfect shade of nylons. How does that sound?"

An eerie, scheming screen shadowed his face and killed the whole thing. The look that made her insides lurch and her heart drown in sudden, unseen tears. Her stomach twisted and turned with guilt. He knew. She knew. But she quickly answered.

"Alright, Toni."

But that night, Toni didn't come back. And in the morning, he still wasn't back. She fixed her hair, got all ready to go out, and he didn't come to get her. She had actually looked forward to going out with Toni. She'd pushed the grimness out of it, and fixed a cute little scene with just she and her sweetheart having a nice outing. When she was refreshing her look and brushing her hair, she heard Alessandro and Toni in a quiet conversation in the hallway...

"I don't know, Al. He told me to be there to get the money, and I had better follow through, or I could forget payment for the Schlinsky murder, this one, the contract, and, perhaps, my life." Toni sighed, with a slight tremor.

Al sucked in a hard breath. "Sounds sketchy. I'll cover for you."

Carmen knew then what was about to take place. She heard something about a "warehouse". And she also knew what warehouse they were referring to. It was "*the*" warehouse where the gang carried out their illicit operations. She also found out who was to be involved. There would be much bloodshed...tonight. Toni didn't even say goodbye. Carmen only heard the creaking of the wooden stairs, provoked by the two sturdy men.

Carmen ran to look for Maria. She sat at the kitchen table with a chipped cup of coffee in one hand, and her head in the other. Her dated clothing showed the poor conditions she'd lived in for so long. Carmen could tell Maria was upset, and when she looked closer, red rims framed her dark eyes. Moisture accompanied the puffiness under them, and if Carmen wouldn't have known better, she would have thought that young, sweet Maria was a sick old woman. Maria looked up at Carmen, a look that showed concern for her friend, her brother, and most importantly, her husband. Carmen thought back over the last four years, all the destruction that had occurred - the murders, the fights, all of it.

Carmen was done. She wasn't about to let it happen again. But first, she had to call someone. She went to the telephone.

"Hello, operator? Get me the police station. Hurry." she spoke.

Maria jumped up and ran to Carmen. "Carmen don't! Please don't! They will be killed! Don't you see?" Maria cried, tears pouring from her eyes.

"Maria, somebody is going to be murdered tonight. We are the only people who know about it and therefore are the only people to keep it from happening."

"Would you rather it be someone you have never met before, someone you don't know, or your man?" Maria protested desperately.

Besides saving an innocent man's life, Toni was not her "man". If Ted was in this situation, it'd be different. Toni was not her lover. She was his prisoner.

Maria's expression softened, and she began to understand. "Yes Carmen, I understand."

Carmen nodded, "Hello? Is this the NYPD? I want to report a murder. It's going to happen tonight." She rattled off the address, quickly spilling out how she had overheard the tip.

After that, she grabbed her raincoat and hat. She hesitated, then reaching into her top dresser drawer, under a slip, she drew out her revolver, and with trembling hands pushed four brand new bullets into the chambers. She stuffed a few extra in her coat pocket for good measure. She had no idea what might happen, or what she may have to do.

"I'm going after them, Maria," Carmen said, looking at her reflection in the mirror, and slipping the shiny gun into her side pocket. She turned to see Maria's face screwed with emotion. Carmen hugged her friend. Rushing down the stairs, she wondered if there really was a God and if He knew about all of this. She half-heartedly muttered a prayer that if He was there, to protect her.

Carmen sneaked into the warehouse and stepped into the shadows, behind a stack of wooden crates. The police were on their way. She peeked her head up and spotted six men in a circle. She recognized three as Prince Romaro, Jacky Vasquez, Guy Sanders; and, of course, Al and Toni. The other, she'd never seen before, and he was pointing a gun. A light from an unknown source cast onto a helpless man tied to a chair, with a cloth in his mouth, fastened around his head. The gun was pointed at him. Carmen stared, aghast, wondering what to do.

Standing up in the dark, she stepped out from behind the boxes. Unable to see a thing, she planted her foot on an unknown object, making a crunch. She gasped as one of the men in the group stepped away to investigate the noise. She tried to step even further back, but there was nowhere to hide, she couldn't run. A hand, which Carmen couldn't see, reached out and clasped onto her elbow. It began pulling her out into view.

"Well, *hello* baby." Jacky hooted, looking her up and down.

"Hiya, pal." Carmen returned sarcastically, wrenching her elbow from his grasp.

"Hey, Toni. Your dame came to pay you a visit. Boy, she must 'a really missed ya."

"Carmen! What are you doing here?" Toni demanded, alarmed.

"I-I-I-her-heard your con-conversation with Al, and-and-well, I got scared, Toni. I-I couldn't just stand by and-and let you get hurt." Carmen struggled with her words.

"What're we gonna do now, boss? She's seen and heard too much." Prince interjected threateningly.

"Well, we'll figure that out later. Right now, I've been given a job to do." Toni raised his gun, only about three feet away from the man sitting in the chair. The man was calm, knowing that there was no going back now. No squirming, no hollering. Keeping his eyes intent on his killer.

"Toni, no!" Carmen found herself screaming. As if her mind had made a decision without her approval, her hand pulled out her revolver. When she finally opened her eyes, Antonio's body was laid out on the floor, and five sets of eyes were upon her. Her hand fell limply to her side with the gun still tightly wrapped in her fingers. Her breath dissipated into a cloud of air outside her body.

Her ears noted a blaring sound outside. Her mind became alert, and her legs broke into a dead run, racing up the stairs, across a loft. Shots scattered around her. She shot through a door, and then down another set of stairs, escaping into an alley. With little recollection of her plight,she found herself back at the apartment.

Breathless from her run and the trek up the stairs, she leaned against the door.

"I killed him, Maria." Carmen breathed.

"Carmen!" Maria's eyes held sheer terror. "Alessandro?"

"He's alright, but the police are there now."

"I must go to him." Maria shakily took her coat from the coat rack and threw her arms into it. "Will you take care of Tina?"

"Maria, I-I don't know if I can do this. I'm so scared-everything happened so fast-I-" Carmen stuttered. Then Maria's pleading eyes convinced her to say yes.

"Good." Maria grabbed a gun from the table. "Carmen, I don't know what's going to happen, but you need to get away, the police will be looking for you. Go to Rosa Vargas' house, she will help you. I will contact you, later." she patted Carmen's hand, and then turned to fetch Tina from her bedroom.

"Goodbye, darling. Mommy has to leave for a while, but I'll be back soon. Okay?" Maria kissed her little girl's cheek

"Okay, Mommy." The little girl smiled. Tears streamed down Carmen's face. Maria was so choked with emotion, she only waved goodbye as she stepped out the door.

Carmen stooped down to Tina's level. "Mommy wants us to go to Grandma Rosa's house. Go get your doll." Carmen was in a panic, she should probably set fire to the apartment, destroy everything. But she didn't care. She wouldn't blame them if they caught her.

When she finally came to her senses, she was closing the alley door to the club. The lights glowed before her. She headed to her dressing room and heard two voices. She recognized one as Ted's but couldn't make out the other. She then found it was a woman's. She put her ear to the door and listened.

It was Kitty, Kitty Manson. She should've known. It was her night. They switched out every other night. Any other time, she would have been fuming at Ted, but now she needed to get her money and run. She had their undivided attention as she opened the door. The redhead had her arms wrapped around Ted's neck, and she shot Carmen a patronizing look with a raised brow. Carmen stopped and stared for just a moment, and then remembered the reason she was there.

Ted pulled Kitty's arms from his neck and pushed her towards the door.

"I'll be there in a minute." Ted murmured, giving Kitty's leg a playful slap. Carmen gritted her teeth, and her hand tensed into a tight fist.

"Well, don't be long, darling." Kitty patted his cheek and then peeked around to look at Carmen, setting her hand on her hip. "Some of us have it, and some us don't. Huh, kid?" turning to close the door, exaggerating the swing of her hips.

Where did she come off calling her "kid"? Carmen rolled her eyes.

"I wasn't expecting to see you tonight, what are you doing here?" Ted asked, trying to brush off the awkward encounter.

"I'm in trouble, Ted. I have the extra you've been giving me hidden here. You know that. I'm skipping town. I'll contact you when I know what I'm going to do," though she had no intention of doing any such thing.

"Baby, please don't leave."

"And what are you going to do about it?" she jammed the flat end of the hammer between the two boards and lifted them up. But she wished she could ram it right into his skull.

"I can find you a place here. You'll be safe. I can come and visit you when I get the chance. Just don't go, honey, please."

She looked up at his eyes, holding back the emotion that had begun to pile in her throat, and soon became evident in her brown eyes. "No, Ted. For one thing: you're married. For two: the police are sniffing every corner of Brooklyn for a woman who murdered a gangster, who was her 'love', and the woman just happens to be 'yours truly'. And for another: I got a kid to protect that isn't even mine, and whose mother is most certainly never coming back. So, the least I can do is take care of her until I can find somebody who can do a better job of it than I. And for one more thing: I've had enough of your games. I thought you were really in love with me. Now I come in here when I'm fleeing for my life to find you in the arms of another woman. I thought it was maybe just me. I thought you maybe didn't even care about your wife anymore. That maybe you would divorce her, and by a very small hope in my heart, marry me."

Carmen could very well see that Ted was carefully sifting out the right words to say to not make her angry, hurt her further, and to make her come crawling back to him on her hands and knees. She dismissed it and continued digging for the key to her box. She found it, and the box, putting everything back exactly as it was.

"Goodbye, Ted. You haven't seen me tonight. The last time you saw me was last night when I came to work. You don't know where I am, or where I'm planning to go." she opened the door to leave.

"I don't know what to say, Carmen." he opened his arms for one final embrace but was refused.

"You don't have to say anything, Ted. It's better if you don't, anyway."

"Wait," Ted shuffled in his pocket, and brought out a wad of money. "Here's for you, honey. Stay safe. Call me. I ... love you, Carmen." Ted kissed her forehead and tucked the money in her coat pocket. She said nothing. If she would have, she wouldn't have been able to wrangle back her emotions.

She emerged from the exit to maneuver her way back to Rosa's little pad by way of only the darkest alleys. But dropping to her knees outside the club, she got sick, and began to sob. He was her weakness, her angel, her strength, her fortress, her victory, her peace. He was her world.

If it would have been any other night but tonight, she would have felt safe in the black remains of night. In the soft soundness of the dark. In the hard coolness of the dank surroundings. But tonight was different. A man had been killed. She'd done it. She would soon be on trial for murder unless she could get to the Mexican border...fat chance of that. She should have gone with Ted. Gone right then. *Heck with you,*

Carmen! You knew this would happen! You got your darn self into this. Why'd you have to fall for him, both of them, either of them? You would have been better off if you'd listened to Mom and Dad. Not come at all. You're only as good as Dad said you were, and always will be. Curse you, Carmen! She scolded herself. The brash words she thought worsened her flood of tears.

When she finally got to Rosa's, she might as well have gone through Canada. It took her long enough. She buzzed the doorbell. A small old woman who was about a foot shorter than Carmen answered the door.

"Come in, my child, come in." the wrinkly woman in gray braids waved. She hobbled to a chair. She was in her late eighties and was skinny and frail. "You poor child! You must go to bed. You have to remember to sleep and stay healthy." she gestured to a chair.

"No, Rosa. Tina and I have to leave. Tonight. We can't risk staying here any longer. We're in danger. And I did something wrong. The least I can do is endure a little weariness for a man I killed... a man I...I thought I loved." she shook her head dismally. "Thank you for the offer, Rosa. I'm sorry to trouble you. I know you will be questioned. I'm...so sorry. I can't tell you how sorry I am." Tears began to slip from her eyes again, and she cupped her mouth with her hands. She'd done such an awful thing. A terrible thing. But there was no going back now.

The little old woman held her close and patted her head when Carmen stooped down. "There now. There now. Don't worry, dear. Everything will come out alright. Just wait and see."

"Oh Rosa, I'm so frightened!"

In a matter of half an hour, Tina and Carmen's meager belongings were stashed in a small, grimy suitcase, and the two were almost four blocks from Rosa's apartment. It had been emotional murder for Carmen to wake the precious little girl from her dreamless sleep at nearly two o'clock in the morning.

Now her little fingers gripped Carmen's index and middle finger and held her ragdoll in the crook of her arm. Carmen had thought it safer, for Rosa's sake, to go a little out of the way of her apartment to catch a cab. They were now closer to the big city, and she gripped Tina closer to her. She stood on the curb for a few minutes before she managed to wave down a taxi. She ducked her features under the visor of her fedora before speaking to the driver.

"Take us across the Brooklyn Bridge, and from there to the cheapest hotel you can find," she told the driver, piling her suitcase and Tina into the seat.

"Okay, lady." he pulled out from the curb and eyed her.

She tried so very hard not to look suspicious, but it was hard to do so without showing her face. A little dark, curly head was placed on her lap. Carmen fingered its gentle, child-like curls. The little girl made a hard yawn. Tears filled Carmen's eyes. *She will never know what happened to her mother.* Carmen thought to herself. Was that a mission, or a promise? Perhaps both.

She looked over the Brooklyn Bridge. The moon was full tonight. Its blueish gleam filled the water with color. A peaceful color, a sad color. Carmen had wanted peace for so long, but all the times before, when she had peace, they were sad times, and they only lasted for a little while. And then Toni's reign had dominated her again, or the Mafia, or poverty, or her work.

Something had always, *always* ruled her. There had always been an iron chain around her neck, her hands, and feet. She never knew why, why she could never hope, never be free. First, it was her parents. She didn't always follow the rules, but when she did, she was still wrong. And then she left, ran away. She thought it would be the answer to all of her problems. And she ran right smack into the arms of a man who controlled her more than her parents ever had. Who had bound her to the mindset that she had no meaning, no purpose. Who only wanted her for what she could give him. From what she'd been taught, that wasn't how a man was supposed to treat a woman. She didn't know, maybe she'd misunderstood.

"This ain't the best-lookin' joint, but it's the cheapest," the taxi driver interrupted her thoughts. She tried her best to pull herself back together. To dry her eyes and speak clearly.

"Thank you, driver." she handed the driver three dollars and fifty cents.

"You all right, Ma'am? I mean you were cryin' on the way here; is there anything I can do?" he looked back at her.

Carmen stiffened, and then hurriedly gathered her things. "No-no thank you. Goodnight."

"Goodnight." the driver called from the window. Carmen pulled Tina to her feet as they climbed the stairs to the rugged hotel.

The desk clerk handed Carmen the keys to the room, and Carmen waddled up two flights of stairs with a sleepy little girl in her arms. She and Tina flopped onto the bed without so much as removing their clothes and getting into something comfortable.

That night, Carmen had a dream, a nightmare. It happened all over again. Another fight with Toni, and then she murdered him. But this time, she stabbed him in their flat, and she felt the ground shake under her when he fell. And she woke when she dreamed she jumped from their fifth-floor apartment to avoid being captured by the police.

When her heart stopped its racing, she dreamt again. This time it was a good dream. She dreamt she was in a little blue house with a white picket fence. She dreamt she knew how to cook, and she was cooking for her two girls, and husband. She never knew who her husband was, his face was...sort of a blur, but it wasn't Toni. This man was the opposite of Toni.

Somehow, one of her daughters was...Tina.

Chapter 4

Carmen woke up with a warm body in her arms. The small figure turned over, yawned, and went back to sleep. Carmen smiled. She wondered what had transpired last night with Maria and Alessandro. Carmen got up and changed out of the old clothes she hadn't shed out of pure exhaustion the night before.

Carmen gently shook the little girl. She told Valentina to get up, and dress. After Carmen helped the little girl into her blue dress, she helped her put on her coat. They started out to a small diner on the other side of the Brooklyn Bridge. Carmen was glad that Tina ate both of the pancakes she ordered. Carmen did not eat anything. Just a small cup of coffee with cream and sugar.

After they left, Carmen needed a haircut, and Tina did too. They found a taxi and a beauty salon. Carmen's hair was at her shoulders, but needed a trim, and was smelly and greasy. Her hair was washed, cut, and dyed a dark brown. She got it curled too. They spent about five hours at the salon. She felt and *looked* like a new woman. Therefore, she must remember to act like it.

They walked a couple of blocks to Macy's. Carmen bought two nice evening dresses, a casual wool suit, blouses, and skirt. She bought a coat too. She bought Tina a nightgown, white buckle shoes, and four dresses with a blue bow for her hair. The little girl had gotten her hair washed, and fixed in little pigtails, just like "Aunt Carmen.". They went back to the hotel room they'd stayed in the night before and dressed up in their new outfits. They packed the rest in the new suitcases they bought.

Next, Carmen and Tina went to check out of the hotel, and from the hotel found transportation to Rosa's friend's house.

Carmen and Tina made their way to a subway station, and Tina clung to her in the mass crowds. Carmen had the paper from one of her dress boxes, and before they left their hotel, she wrapped her gun in it. Passing a trash can while waiting for the next subway, Carmen gently, unsuspectingly slipped the gun into it. She breathed a sigh. She was rid of that piece of evidence.

They could walk to Giorgia's from the subway. Carmen looked the little girl in the eye when they were standing on Giorgia's doorstep.

"Tina, listen to me." the little girl's eyes met the woman's. "Tina, what I'm about to say is very important. Grandma Rosa, who gave us this address, told the woman who lives here that I am married, and you are my little girl. You are now to address me as 'Mommy'. Okay?"

The girl looked puzzled. Tears started to drip from her eyes.

"But you're not my mommy, Aunt Carmen." the little girl choked out.

"I have to be for now," Carmen felt like a hard-nosed stepmother. "Please call me 'Mommy' while we're here, Tina. That's our only chance. You'll understand it one day. Now, smile."

Tina did as she was told. "Yes, Mommy."

"Good. Now come on." Tina clutched her ragdoll to her little chest as she stood, holding Carmen's hand.

Butterflies arose in Carmen's stomach when she buzzed the door. A stout woman in a gray-haired bun answered the door.

"Oh, my dear! You must be Mrs. Benetzi! And this must be your little girl! Oh, please, please, please come in!" Giorgia ushered them in. She had a thick Italian accent that showed.

"Thank you for letting us stay with you, Miss Giorgia," Carmen said, stepping into the house.

"No trouble at all. Let me take your coat." she slipped Carmen's coat from her shoulders, and Tina's too. "You are brave, child. Rosa told me all about it. Poor girl losing your husband. So tragic. I'm sorry, my dear." the woman brought her in for a close hug.

The woman showed her to the upstairs guest room, and then took Tina downstairs for some milk and cookies. She told her that dinner would be at six, and it was four-thirty now. She said her grandson would be there for dinner. When Giorgia closed the door, Carmen started a mental breakdown.

The world had fallen on her shoulders. How she wished that somebody could hold her, even for just a moment. *Ted!* She thought. *You should've taken care of him too. Why didn't you? You still had the gun in your pocket.* Her heart begged. But she knew how it felt to be close to Ted, to hold him in her arms. How could she wish to kill a man as good as he? But she reminded herself that he wasn't hers to claim. What would she do next, if she could manage to hide in the shadows, and stay clear of the cops?

What about the kid? She couldn't do this for the rest of her life. Carmen wasn't about to run off and leave her here. She'd been given a job to do, and she was going to do it. But she hadn't heard from Maria. Carmen knew she was dead, they both were dead. And it gave her a sinking feeling in her stomach. She'd killed Toni, and she'd killed them all.

Carmen figured she'd go back into her life as a gun moll, eventually. Or perhaps she would venture back home. Maybe she'd killed one Toni just to get back with a dozen others like him.

What else was she worth? She'd give a dime to the first person to make up some ridiculous excuse. And what of Ted? Could he forget about Kitty, and be happy with Carmen? And even then, could she love him again after this?

After an hour, Carmen was beginning to think she was feeling sorry for herself. Pulling herself back together, she started dressing for the evening. She picked out a black dress with a v-neck and shapely figure that flattered her body, with her usual black stilettos. She trotted down the stairs. She came to the kitchen and was helping to fix dinner when the door buzzed.

"Dear Carmen, would answer that? It's my grandson." Giorgia asked politely.

"Certainly," Carmen replied, putting down the salad. She marched down the long, wide hallway. She was expecting to open the door to a boy, no higher than her waist, but what stood before her in the open door was no boy.

A man, about the size of Toni, in a casual suit, and fedora.

"Hello." Carmen shyly managed to say, shocked by the overly-handsome man.

"Hello. Are you Mrs. Benetzi?" He asked, referring to Toni's last name. Their eyes met for a long moment, Carmen hoped she wasn't just imagining the spark she saw in his eye.

"Yes. And you are?"

"Steve. Giorgia's grandson," he said, but stopped, obviously taken by the woman. "May I come in?" he asked, shaking away her trance.

"Oh yes, I'm sorry." she stepped back from the door. She was very embarrassed when she realized she had been staring at him with her mouth half-way open.

*That's her **grandson**?* She thought. Carmen hadn't realized the sudden heat rising around her neck. Being the kind of woman she was, she had to practically chain herself to the wall, to keep from flinging herself onto this man.

"That's alright. Where is she?" Steve asked.

"In the kitchen, may I take your coat?" Carmen asked, holding her hands out.

Her real ploy was to see what the man's arms looked like.

"Sure, thanks." he handed her his hat and coat. "Nonna! Your favorite grandson is here!"

"Oh! My Stevie!" Giorgia hollered, running from the kitchen. She gave him a kiss on his cheek. They started into the kitchen.

He was trying to be the nonchalant guy, that should be his normal manner; but he had sneaked a second look at the beautiful woman, that Carmen didn't notice.

Yes, he does look strong, and handsome.

Carmen checked in the mirror. Her brown hair suited her, and she was going to make the most of being an impressionate "new Carmen". She fixed her curls to better shape her face and gave her dress a tug, anxious to be in the company of this strikingly gorgeous man. She walked to the kitchen, but before she opened the door, she heard a conversation between Steve and his grandmother.

"She is pretty, yes?" Giorgia prodded.

"Ah, Nonna, you're my only sweetheart." Steve kissed his grandmother's cheek.

"As you newfangled Americans say, 'Lay off that.' You need a woman, my Stevie."

"Ah, I can live without 'em, I'm happy living the way I am. I don't have to tie myself down to just one, play the field. Besides, you know I kinda lost my hope for ever loving a woman again after that fiasco in the Pacific."

"You can't say you don't find her attractive! I know the woman left you brokenhearted, but you have another life now, Stevie. That happened a long time ago. Now, look at you. Successful, happy, good-looking. But alone. You need somebody to help you, love you. You told me how you want children, someday. You need a wife, Stevie." Giorgia said, saddened.

Steve said no more, he knew the old sage was right, he was lonely. He gave her shoulder a tight squeeze.

So, he is single. Carmen silently noted. Not that it mattered. She had now baited her trap. After hearing the exchange between he and his grandmother, she knew the "marrying kind" was what he was looking for. She now marched through the kitchen door, making a good first impression as the lady that she was trying to be. Upon entering the kitchen, the grandmother and grandson looked at the woman. Carmen flashed an innocent, toothy smile.

Chapter 5

Carmen picked up Tina and placed her under the covers. She recalled the events of the last couple of hours. She had gotten more acquainted with Steve. Though she could have done without the part when he revealed his high position with the NYPD. He had been promoted to chief investigator of the homicide unit two years ago. Her first notion was to high-tail it out of there, but her heart told her not to give up on this man quite yet ... and, it would look suspicious.

"Carmen, what have you gotten yourself into?" she whispered aloud to herself.

Her love interests since she came to New York could not have been more different. Yet there was something oddly familiar about Steve, from long ago. The world she came from, before New York. The kind of man she'd envisioned herself with before. A nice man. Well brought up. The man her father was, but whom she had resented, and escaped from. He didn't immediately grab her like a wolf.

She shook the thought from her mind.

She was now downstairs, having coffee with Steve and Giorgia in the parlor.

~

Steve's mind kept drifting to the case laid fresh on his desk just this morning. He had been off duty the night before to go to a buddy's wedding. He went to the crime scene later that night. Seven bodies, he found out later. A bloodthirsty killing. A man was arrested. He wouldn't say what his name was. Steve had interrogated him until he could no longer stand it, and had gotten nowhere with the thug. Steve was not good at questioning, and he didn't like it. That was part of his problem. But before the fella clammed up completely, Steve had managed to eke out of him something about a mysterious woman who was responsible for one of the killings, thus saving the man's life. He claimed to know nothing about her, including her name.

~

"Are you worried about something, my boy?" Giorgia asked her grandson.

"No, I'm alright, Nonna," Steve assured. He was not to discuss the case with anybody just yet.

Carmen wanted to quickly interject another subject but was afraid she'd give herself away. Her throat was so dry, she couldn't speak anyway.

"Did Tina go to sleep easily?" Giorgia asked Carmen.

"Oh, yes. Fine." Carmen squeaked. Her mind thought how peacefully Tina was sleeping, considering the last twenty-four hours. To avoid the topic of conversation put on her, she complimented Giorgia on the dinner.

Steve, in the habit of asking questions, proceeded to ask Mrs. Benetzi.

"I don't note a New Yorker accent, have you been here long, Mrs. Benetzi?"

Carmen had to think up an answer quickly, a good answer, without giving herself away. "I'm originally from Kansas, but I came here for a visit five years ago, and haven't gone back home since. My parents didn't even meet my husband, nor have they met their granddaughter." she lied.

"So, do you think you'll go back to Kansas, now?" Giorgia asked. Carmen was, again, hesitant.

"Forgive me for being so personal." Giorgia soothed, knowing it hadn't been long since the girl had lost her husband.

False tears gathered in Carmen's eyes, though they were somewhat real. "I'm not sure of my plans yet. It all happened so suddenly."

"Of course, my dear. Take all the time you need. You may stay here while you think out the best plan for you and your daughter."

Carmen's glance shifted to Steve, whose eyes were upon her. His glance showed admiration for this brave woman. He cleared his throat as he realized he was staring at her all the while.

"Excuse me, I have a case I must put some effort into tonight." Steve stood.

"Goodbye, Nonna." Steve pecked Giorgia's cheek.

"Goodbye, Stevie; stay safe, my boy. See you at church, tomorrow?"

"Sorry, Nonna. Don't think I can this weekend. This case is important, it was lucky for me I could get away this long." Steve patted her shoulder.

"I will see you to the door, Steve." Carmen set her coffee cup down and stood.

Giorgia sneaked a wink at Steve. He responded with a quick, but subtle grin.

As they exited the parlor, he put a gentle hand on her arm with sincere compassion and said. "I'm sorry for your loss."

"Thank you," Carmen replied softly.

"Will I see you again?" Steve asked hopefully.

"I hope so. You are nice company. I will be staying here for a couple weeks until I decide what to do. Anyway, your grandmother will see to it." Carmen said with a chuckle. Steve took her hand. She wrapped her hand around his. His grip was strong but gentle. He was slow to release it. Carmen sucked in a breath. She'd never been treated so gently, not even by Ted.

"Yeah, she will. Well, goodbye." Steve smiled warmly, opening the door.

"Goodbye." Carmen shut the door behind him.

Chapter 6

Oh, stop it, Steve! He silently scolded himself. His mind continued to drift to the woman whose company he'd just left. She'd been at his grandmother's house for almost a week and a half, now. They had gone on five dates already, and everything was moving along nicely. He was really beginning to fall in love with this woman.

"Chief! I just got a new scoop," said Joe Frager, who was Steve's right-hand man on most cases, and a close friend.

"What's that?" Steve asked.

"There was another woman in with the gang. The fella that we found out was the ringleader, she's his girl. She was a little more than a girl, if you know what I mean, but that's not the point. We talked to neighbors. We have a good description of her. Quite a dame. She worked at that club down the street from where we found the bodies. Her name's Carmen, according to the club owner. We searched her apartment. Nothing too exciting there besides a couple of dresses, that's how we found the club. That's about all, Sir." Joe stated.

"Did you find out the fella's name?" Steve asked.

"Oh, yeah, Toni Benetzi."

"What?" Steve asked, mesmerized. *Benetzi.* She couldn't have anything to do with it. Must just be a coincidence.

"Toni Benetzi. What's wrong, Chief?" Joe was now very concerned for his friend. "Oh, I was meaning to ask you, how'd it go with the, uh, dame last night?" Joe asked with a sly smile. Steve was thinking, rubbing his chin.

"I don't know, yet," Steve stated, he got up from his chair, and grabbed his coat and hat. He drove to his grandmother's and knocked on the door, trying to contain the reason he was really here.

"Hi, Nonna." Steve stepped into the house.

"Hello, Steve. What a nice surprise." Giorgia's face lit up.

"Is Trudy here?" Steve asked, speaking "Mrs. Benetzi's" given first name.

"Yes, she is upstairs with the little girl. Do you have something to tell her?" Giorgia raised an eyebrow. Thinking he might "pop the question".

"Maybe. Nonna, would you come to the kitchen with me?" Steve was trying to calm his racing heart. He might have to do the most unpleasant job ever performed. The woman was innocent until proven guilty, but he still suspected her. His conscience was hovering over him. He had a gut-wrenching feeling inside him. He had his job.

He could not divulge anything. Not yet. At the kitchen table, they sat.

"Stevie, what is bothering you, my boy?" Giorgia asked, concerned.

"Oh, never mind that, Nonna. I wanted to ask you, what do you know about this woman?"

"I know nothing, really, just what I told you. Rosa, my good friend, told me she had a friend that lived in Brooklyn, in the same apartment building as she. The girl needed a place to stay. She-Trudy-had a little girl. Her husband had died only a few weeks before."

"Uh-huh. What did Trudy tell you about her husband's death?" Steve asked, crossing his arms.

"She's not talked about it. I didn't want to pry. I figured, if she wanted to talk about it, she would. She has kept to herself, really. Why do you ask, Stevie?" Giorgia answered.

"Oh, I was just curious. You know me, prying into other people's affairs is what I get paid for. Just wondering, Nonna." Steve brushed it off. But he was getting hungrier to sniff out this woman's history with every word Giorgia uttered.

"What I really came here for is to see if I could snatch Trudy away for a couple hours this evening."

"Ah! I knew you were going to say that, my boy. You are very romantic. She will be lucky if she catches you. And you will be a lucky man, too. Yes?"

Giorgia asked, hopefully. Steve cleared his throat. "Yeah. I guess so." he rubbed his neck.

"Well get up there before I'm too old to enjoy my great grandchildren. Go!" she swung a dish towel at his back end and pushed him out of the kitchen.

Carmen and Tina came down the stairs. Carmen's face lit up when she saw Steve. But she noticed darkness in his eyes, instead of a sparkle she usually saw. It puzzled Carmen. She had no idea what to do. She calmly, and sweetly pecked his cheek. He tried to smile as best he could.

"Shall we go in to help Giorgia with dinner?" Carmen asked, relieved he had shown a smile.

"Well, I was wondering if you wanted to go out to dinner tonight?" Steve asked, putting his hands in his pockets.

"Why, that would be wonderful. Just let me fix myself up, first." Carmen agreed.

"Alright," Steve answered sweetly. She walked up the stairs, not taking her eyes from him.

They were seated at their table. They made small talk while looking at the menu. Carmen and Steve gave their orders to the waiter, then Steve crossed his arms on the table.

"We've been seeing each other for a while now, and yet I know very little about you. Tell me about yourself."

Carmen fidgeted. She didn't know what to say. She decided to take the safe road. She knew this moment would come. She had played the situation in her mind countless times, and now that it was here, she had no idea what to say.

"What can I say, my hometown isn't very interesting. I was raised in a small farm community in Kansas. My parents were Christians, I've always been a strong believer in God." she lied. "I believe that He's the only reason I didn't attempt suicide ... after my husband died." Carmen sniffed and lowered her head, as if to express her grief. She was getting good at lying. She felt awful telling such lies, but she had to stay safe. God had started to open her mind; she was finding herself wanting Him, but was unsure how to go about it. She was still very afraid.

"Now, there, there, Trudy. Don't cry. I'm sorry it's been so hard for you the last few weeks, but it will all get better." he soothed, though he was sure it was all a gag.

They had enjoyed their meal. The conversation of their pasts was cut off. They were now strolling by a lake outside of the restaurant.

It was now his job to find out more about this case. But he had to be careful. If he revealed too much, and she wasn't the woman, he would lose his job. If he told her too much, and she was the woman, he would have to act fast, before she ran.

"How's your life been since New York? I mean, what's happened?" Steve got the courage to ask. He maneuvered the sentence carefully.

"Well, it's like I said. I came here on a trip, and I never went back. I had my daughter Tina, one year after we were married. We were so happy, and then…" Carmen's face screwed up, into a fake, painful sob.

"I'm sorry, I didn't mean to pry." Steve excused himself.

"It's okay. It helps me to talk about him." Carmen's face returned to normal, much like a spoiled child who'd guilt-tripped her parents into what she wanted. The action was too hasty, Carmen should have realized that. Steve noted it. He knew then she was lying.

"What was your husband's name?" he asked.

"His name?" she confirmed. She hadn't thought of that. "Fred." she quickly lied.

Steve also noticed how she had paused, and then quickly spewed out the name. Steve got up the nerve to ask her the one question that would answer it all. His chest heaved.

"Carmen." he said, flatly. Her head turned.

She gasped quietly. She realized what she had just done. They slowly walked to the car. They were silent on the drive to Giorgia's house.

He knew she wouldn't try to run. She had a child with her. What would she do with her? He walked her to the door. They didn't say goodnight.

Chapter 7

Carmen lay in bed, unable to sleep. Her mind cranked her more and more awake. Her insides turned. She'd been restless ever since she'd laid down. Her mind drifted. *Will he still love me? Will I be good enough after he finds out all that I've done, that I killed a man? What will happen to Tina? What will happen to me? Do I have only hours to live? What if I don't know what to say at the trial? Will he forgive that I have been with two other men? What does God think about me? If I can't find mercy in anyone else, can I find mercy with Him? Will I ever know the comfort of a man's arms again? What about the murder?*

All of this was too much for Carmen to bear. She jumped from her bed and raced to the telephone at the end of the stair.

"Hello, operator, would you get me the NYPD, Homicide Department?" she spoke into the receiver. "Is this the Homicide Department? I want to speak to the chief, Steve Comochello."

~

On the other end of the line, Steve was wrenched from his sleep.

"There's some dame on the phone, some dame by the name of *Trudy*," Joe said with a charismatic drawl to the name *Trudy*. Steve immediately stood, in his disheveled hair and loose necktie, and ran to the phone. He had slept at the office that night. He knew she would confess, sooner or later. He cleared his throat of sleepiness.

"Hello." he croaked.

"Steve! Steve! Come to Giorgia's house right away, I've got something to tell you. I need you, Steve." she pleaded.

"Alright, I'm on my way. I'll be there in twenty minutes."

"Oh, do hurry!" she wept. He hung up the phone.

His friend waited for him to report what had been said. Joe knew nothing of what Steve suspected.

"What? She havin' sweet dreams, and you happen to be in 'em?" Joe laughed.

"Ah, shut up." Steve waved his hand in dismissal.

"Stevie's in love! Stevie's in love!"

"Get out of my way." Steve pushed by him to get to the door.

"Something else you wanna tell me, boy?"

"*Sono innamorato*. Figure it out." Steve flipped Joe's hat over his eyes.

"Hey!" Joe hollered, putting his fists up, ready to fight. Steve closed the door in his face.

"Gee, I wish I could find a dame like that, and fall in love that quick." Joe said to himself and shrugged his shoulders.

Steve stood on the step.

"If You make this hard for her, I'll never speak to You, again." he said, pointing to the sky that was releasing buckets of rain. Before he could knock on the door, Carmen threw it open and hung on his shoulders. Just like all the femme fatales do in the movies. She was sobbing uncontrollably.

"Your name is Carmen Everett." he said flatly, shuffling into the house, and closing the door. "You were involved with Toni Benetzi. But you had no part in the crimes. Tina is not your daughter. She belongs to Maria and Alessandro Conti. You are not Trudy Benetzi." Steve said through tears stinging his eyes, gripping the shoulders of the woman that clung so tightly to him. She slipped from his arms to the floor, holding her face in her hands.

"I have also carried on with a married man." she blubbered. "The owner of a nightclub. I'm not the Christian woman I made out to be. That's why I came to New York, to get away from my parents badgering me about religion, among other things. I have shut God out, completely. But I have seen what your God can do. I want to be like the people at your church that I have seen, God breathing life into them every time they walk into the sanctuary. I want to be that person and need to be. Now, more than ever. Help me, Steve, I need you!" she sobbed. He bent down to her level.

"I will help you, but don't say any more. I love you, as much as I always have. I need you; I see that. And I have a job - you know I have a job. I have to take you in, but I'll be with you. I may have to question you, so please don't hate me. And I will try my hardest to get you out of this mess."

She nodded, but couldn't make out words.

"Good." he got her to her feet. They closed and locked the door. Steve left a note saying he would be back in the morning and would explain it all then.

He took hold of her arm. Tightly, uncomfortably. He was just trying to get into the mentality that he was supposed to be putting this woman in jail. For a murder. But it was no less saddening to Carmen.

The windshield wipers swished back and forth vigorously. It poured, and bolts of lightning crashed across the sky.

"Carmen, darling." he planted his right hand on her knee as she stared blankly out the window.

"Don't. Please, Steve." she tore her knee from his reach.

"Carmen, you told me you understood."

"I do Steve! I just don't want this to be any harder, for either of us, than it has to be." she sniffed. "Steve, I-I'm sorry I lied to you, I-"

She was cut off.

"Carmen, don't say any more. I know now you were just trying to protect yourself, and the child. I know you feel bad, but don't say any more. Things are sticky enough as it is. When we get to the station, I want you to act just like any other suspect I might be questioning. If we act like we're together, the D.A. is going to pull every trick in the book to get you behind bars." Steve breathed.

"Alright. Steve, no matter what's happened before, no matter what's said, remember that I love you. That's all in my past. I don't care about it anymore. Remember that, Steve. Promise me." Carmen snuggled up to Steve's shoulder.

"I'll remember it, Carmen. I promise." he put his arm around her shoulder and kissed her forehead.

"I'm s-scared stiff, Steve." she whimpered, trying hard to hide the crack in her voice.

"Don't be, honey. This is all going to come out alright. And after it's all blown over, we can forget about it."

It was going to come out alright. It had to come out alright if she was ever going to have half a chance with Steve. And she already had his promise that he would be there to pick her up if she fell.

~

Steve didn't see Carmen as a killer. A real killer, but most likely self-defense; or protecting someone else. He felt awfully sorry for her. But he knew it might very well be just because he was in love with her. More than anything in the world, he wanted this woman in his life. For the rest of his life. No matter what she might be accused of.

Chapter 8

They arrived at the station, and Steve checked her in at the front desk. He then took her arm and escorted her back to his office. He wrapped her in his arms once more and gave her a comforting kiss. He then showed her a warm smile to put her at ease.

She felt her tense muscles relax. She felt comfortable now. He showed her to a chair and told her to "please sit". He now leaned back on his desk and crossed his arms.

"So, let's start from the beginning." Steve prompt. She then recounted every step she took from the time she left her hometown.

It was now three fifteen in the morning, but she remembered everything, as clear as day. She told her love how disgusting she thought the Kansas dust was, and how exciting, and adventurous the concrete jungles of New York had seemed. She had just turned eighteen in February. It had been only the beginning of April when she left. She knew absolutely nothing about life. She pawned her jewelry to get the money to get here. She went hungry for three days until she reached New York. When she got there, she'd bought a newspaper, and looked for hotels and apartments in the area. In her search, she noticed a job advertisement at The Hot Spot, in Brooklyn.

"It was in a pretty abandoned district," she recalled. Ted was there, and she fell in love with him at first sight, as he confessed he had with her. He hired her as a singer, and her first performance was that night. She stayed at the club for a couple months, living out of her dressing room. Soon, she started her affair with Ted, knowing well ahead of time he was married. It was something she had never thought about before, now was the perfect time to stop worrying what people thought, because she was free. Then shortly, she moved in with Toni.

"I started to like the idea more, and more." Carmen continued. "At first, it was a little girl's fantasy, living as a real gun moll, like in all the movies. But I soon realized it was much less glamorous than I thought. He turned into the opposite man I thought he was. He would get quite violent, especially after he'd been drinking."

By now, it was impossible to crawl out from the hole she dug herself because she knew too much about Toni's gang. He would have killed her.

"I don't know, maybe that would have been better than to have been buried in the mess I'm in now."

"Don't ever say that." Steve took her hand. "Everything will be okay." She then started to explain the night she had killed Toni.

"Wait, don't say any more," Steve asked.

"I have to, Steve. I can't hold it in any longer." Carmen pleaded. She told about how Toni had acted suspiciously all week, and how she overheard the conversation in the hallway.

"I had to call the police, Steve. I was so fed up. I was done. I didn't want him to hurt anyone else, and I was done with him hurting me."

And then she told him of the episode in the warehouse, and tears sprang to her eyes.

"I didn't want to kill him, Steve! I didn't mean to kill him!" she sobbed. Steve pulled up a chair next to her and put an arm around her trembling shoulders.

"There, there." he soothed. "Of course, you didn't."

She went on about the money hidden in the box at the club, Rosa's house, and then the taxi ride to the hotel. She told him of the makeover she had gotten, what her natural hair color was, and that she had spent a lot of money on redoing herself.

"Well, that's about the gist of it," she explained. Steve let out a long sigh. It was now almost six thirty in the morning.

"Can I get you some coffee?" Steve asked groggily while yawning.

"Oh yes. Please." she stretched and followed him to the other side of the room to the coffee pot. After it was brewed, they sipped on their cups.

"Here we are, just like married folks. Having our coffee before work." Carmen smiled thoughtfully.

"When this whole thing blows over, I wouldn't have a second thought about a thing like that." Steve told her. She tipped her head and smiled. She knew he was serious.

"You have the right to one phone call," he stated.

"I have nobody to call. You and God are on my side. That's all that really matters." she said.

"Come with me." Steve pulled her to a chair, grabbed a Bible from inside his desk drawer, and sat across from her.

He flipped to Romans 3:23. He read, *"For all have sinned, and fall short of the glory of God."* He took her two delicate hands in his large, masculine paws. "Carmen. That means we have all sinned, everyone on this Earth has sinned. Not just you, and not just me." The words brought her comfort. He then prayed that God would immerse her in His glory. He did.

She prayed aloud, "My Father God. I love You more than anything else, for the first time. I'm sorry for disappointing You. I need You, oh God." Carmen immediately felt like she belonged to Him. She wanted to please Him.

She and Steve drifted to sleep, with her head cradled in his lap. She felt true peace. No more running away, no more hiding. It was good that she didn't have to keep everything to herself. For the first time, and it felt wonderful.

Chapter 9

Joe strode into the homicide department to the front desk.

"Jessica, Steve come in here yet?" he asked the woman at the desk.

"He's been in his office since three fifteen, with a lady," she replied.

Joe grinned mischievously. "Gosh, he's sure a lucky guy to have a dame like Trudy," Joe said thoughtfully.

"The dame's name wasn't Trudy," Jessica said, peering over her glasses, winking at Joe.

"The boy's playing the field, huh?"

"Depends on the way you look at it. The dame's Carmen," she replied.

When Jessica said "Carmen" Joe's jaw dropped, and his head hung. "Holy cats!" Joe rubbed his face.

"What are you so worried about?" she asked. Jessica knew Steve could take care of himself.

"Worried about? Worried about! Do you know that our one homicide chief is in there, and she probably killed him, and all the evidence along with him the second they closed that door? And what's more, girly, you're the one who let her do it!"

"For heaven's sake Joe, calm down! He knew what he was doing. He brought her here." Jessica assured.

"Alright. But I'm going in there, and don't you try to stop me." he waved his finger at her.

"Who's stopping you?"

"Free tonight, honey?" Joe asked, raising his brow.

"Still not free. Go be a hero." Jessica waved her pencil at him.

"If I keep getting turned down by dames like you, I'll never get married." Joe sulked.

"You won't get married anyway." Jessica winked at him once more. She took her eyes from him and looked down at her paperwork.

Joe barged into the room where Carmen and Steve were sleeping in their chairs. He stopped short.

"Trudy." he murmured under his breath. He started to slowly back out of the room. He tripped on a chair, and as he tried to catch himself, kicked the wastepaper basket. He jolted the couple from their sleep.

Steve looked at Joe, and with a sigh said, "What do you want now, Joe?"

"All my questions are answered," Joe stated, with a sly smile. He backed up and blindly searched for the doorknob.

"Carmen, Joe. Joe, Carmen." Steve introduced.

"Ma'am." he lifted his fedora and exited the room. Steve looked at Carmen.

"That's my always discreet and steady sidekick, Joe Frager," he said, sarcastically.

Chapter 10

That afternoon, Carmen met with a court-appointed attorney, Dan Fletcher. He was wonderfully understanding. He listened carefully and patiently to her raw sob story.

Witnesses, though few and far between, were rounded up and questioned. These included Ted and Rosa. The man that Carmen had saved that night, was being pounded harder than ever to get him to talk. They'd gotten little prodded out of him, for he was a hooligan himself.

Over the course of several days, Carmen, her attorney, and a representative of the District Attorney's office met to discuss the death of Antonio Benetzi.

Because of lacking evidence, Carmen Everett was released, scot-free, on February 18, 1952. She nearly fainted with relief, stepping out of the office.

That evening, Steve, and Carmen, and Valentina went to dinner. After the meal, Carmen, Steve, and Tina went back to Giorgia's place. Giorgia had gone to a church meeting, so they had the house all to themselves. Carmen and Steve sat on the couch. Steve scooped the child onto his lap, tickling her small body. She gave out the giggles only little girls make.

"Did you have a good time tonight, Tina?" Steve asked, cradling her.

"Yes. It was fun." the little girl responded. "Tickle me again, Uncle Stevie!" she asked. The man did as she requested, opening another flood of giggles.

~

Carmen smiled at the beautiful scene she had never imagined she would enjoy so much. Everything had come out alright, just as Steve promised. And she had a lot more to look forward to, now that it was all over. Sometimes she wondered if she'd really be able to live up to Steve's expectations of her, and even if she did for a while, would she forever? But Steve and God would put their trust in her, and give her the strength to do it.

~

Steve was happy. He didn't know when he'd last been so happy.

Carmen was a one-in-a-million woman. Gems like that didn't come around very often. Her heart was bigger than the world they lived in. And she didn't deserve any of what she'd gone through. But she was free now. He felt proudest that he'd been instrumental in doing it. He would try his very best to give her everything she could ever want. The more masculine side of him pointed out that she was quite a looker, too.

Valentina was another wonderful thing to marrying Carmen. She already called him "Uncle Steve", and it felt absolutely grand. He was hoping that in the near future she might call him "Daddy".

God had once again intervened, this time concerning the fate of this precious orphaned child. With the absence of any other known family, the judge saw fit to immediately grant Carmen full custody of Valentina, by-passing the conventional due process of the courts. His compassionate heart convinced him this was in the best interest of the child who had already suffered enough trauma and loss in her brief span.

June 1956

Four Years Later...

"Mommy!" Tina called. "Mommy" was all Carmen heard anymore. *"Mommy"* this, *"Mommy"* that.

"Ouch!" Carmen poked her eye with her mascara brush when she jumped at her name being called. "What is it, Tina?" she sighed.

"Susie dumped a bag of flour on her head." the eight-year-old pointed toward the kitchen.

"Oh for goodness' sake!" Carmen jumped up.

"Mommy, you have that black stuff all over your face!" she giggled.

Carmen looked in the mirror, sure enough.

"Oh, that's not funny! We're not going to be ready when daddy comes home from the store!"

Carmen raced out of her bedroom to find her three-year-old on the countertop, completely covered from head to toe, in flour.

"You little monster, how did you get up there!" Carmen scolded, lifting the girl off the counter. "Oh, what a mess! Tina, you had better take her outside, and try to get the most of this stuff shaken off of her, while I find her some clothes."

Tina did as she was told, and soon, Carmen and family were ready to go on their routine Saturday picnic in Central Park.

"Daddy, Daddy, Daddy! This place, this place! Right here! Stop!" Tina practically flew out of the car at the screech of tires.

"Whoa! Hey! Don't go too far!" Steve hollered at Tina, running across the parking lot. Steve and Carmen unloaded the back of the car, and then the two girls found a place to sit down.

Carmen positioned her full skirt around her. This was her peaceful time. Steve would play with the little girls, and Carmen could look up at the sky, and listen to the birds.

This week she would busy herself with preparations for a dinner she would be giving for her new neighbors that had moved down the street a couple of weeks ago. And taking Tina to her ballet lessons on Thursday, that she enjoyed so much. Also, preparing a Sunday school lesson for the little children at church, and taking care of the two beautiful jewels that had entered her life, what seemed a lifetime ago.

Her previous life hardly entered her mind any longer. It was almost completely forgotten. Every once in a while, she would have a nightmare about Toni hitting her, or something as such. But Steve would wrap her in his arms and hold her through the night. Sometimes she would remember Ted, and her guilty conscience would prick at her. And then she would remember that her God had washed that away years ago. Steve had forgiven her, and she might forgive herself one day. But she was still healing.

Steve was such a help. He played with the girls in the evenings, giving Carmen a chance to finish cleaning up the house or read a book.

Her dream that she'd had the night of Toni's death came true. Right down to the blue color of the house, and the white picket fence, and she learned to cook. And the dreamy man she had been married to, and Tina.

She had visited her parents, shortly after she and Steve were married. Her mother cried for joy, and her father too, while apologizing. She made frequent trips back home, especially now that she had her own daughter. It felt so nice to have made amends with her family.

Carmen's thoughts were interrupted when she caught Steve winking at her from across the park.

~

She waved at him, and he smiled. He put his finger up to his lips, gesturing her to be quiet. Carmen winked and nodded. He was hiding behind a bush with his little Susie in his arms. They were hiding from Tina. She was the seeker this time.

"Daddy, Sissy, where are youuu?" Tina picked up a branch a bush away from them.

They'd come a very long way in the last four years. Life before Carmen seemed like a vague fog now. Being lonely was a distant memory. She'd made him so happy. Sure, it hadn't been palaces and rainbows all this time. They'd had their moments. But it had been as close to paradise as he could get. God had been gracious to them, and whatever happened to them, they could face it together, under God's loving care.

"I found you! I found you both!" Tina managed to wiggle her way into Steve's lap alongside Susie.

And so... you know the drill. A girl with a terrible past finds the guy of her dreams under unusual circumstances, the two fall in love, and all live happily ever after.

Well, it was just like that for this beautiful bottle blonde, Carmen Comochello, this damsel in distress. No, she has not changed from the gal you met four years ago. The same shade of red lips, the same nails, the same girl. But this is a happy, carefree Carmen.

This early summer night, the breeze ever so gently touches the red tea roses that Carmen prides herself in planting and caring for. The children are asleep, and Carmen and Steve sit on the porch, the radio echoing quietly inside the house, its comforting trumpets blowing. A book is nestled in Carmen's hand and a cigarette in Steve's. The neighbor's cat stops in to bid the couple sweet dreams, and Mr. and Mrs. Connors' car buzzes by with a little honk to say hello. The city lights can be seen a distance from the house, and all is still in the little neighborhood. Oh, Carmen. Sweet, beautiful Carmen.

You've got yourself a beautiful life.

The End

Acknowledgements

Thank you, to my lovely sister, Teryn, for creating the cover of my book. Thank you for your encouragement to keep going, no matter how hard it gets. I love you dearly, God bless.

Thanks, Mom, for all of your ideas, and for allowing me to follow you around from room to room with my computer when I've been confused and stuck while writing this book, and for encouraging me to pursue my newest burning passion. You are loved and appreciated beyond all thinking.

Thank you, Grandpa, for introducing me to old movies. I would not be the same without you.

And Grandma, for letting me read to you my new little triumphs.

Thank you, cousins, (little sisses!) Lanie and Ellie, for all of your support, hoorahs, sighs, laughs, and gasps, while letting me show you where my heart truly belongs.

Thank you, Mr. Phil Frick, for your help and encouragement.

Thank you, my beloved friend Sarah, for your encouragement, and excitement for me. Thank you for inspiring me to be strong, square my shoulders, and walk with my head held high. You are so strong and beautiful yourself. You light up my world, and so many others.

Thanks, Tina (my cat), for keeping me company and letting me talk to you, and for being the inspiration for the little girl in my story.

Thank you to the reviewers and editors of this book. Without you, this book would not have been published.

My Lord and Savior, thank You most of all for my talents and interests. You made me who I'm supposed to be, and are one reason that I wrote this book. You redeem the most hopeless people and make them whole again, by Your grace. I will try my hardest to listen and fulfill what You placed me here to do.

The Story Behind the Story

Last year, on the morning of July 30th, 2018, I woke up with the name *Carmen...* on my mind. I couldn't shake it. I immediately jumped out of bed, and right away, I knew every detail of the story. I ran upstairs, picked my computer up from my desk, and began to type.

I'm not exactly sure what inspired the idea of writing the story of a murder, but I guess it's from all of the 1940s and '50s noir, crime movies I've watched. It was also the idea of redemption, from a mixed-up life in which a lost woman finds herself trapped.

In my own way, I have also been given a second chance. When I was four months away from turning five years old, I received a life-giving, triple-organ transplant that saved my life. God worked it out perfectly, and it was a test. With struggles overcome, I have learned to trust God in everything.

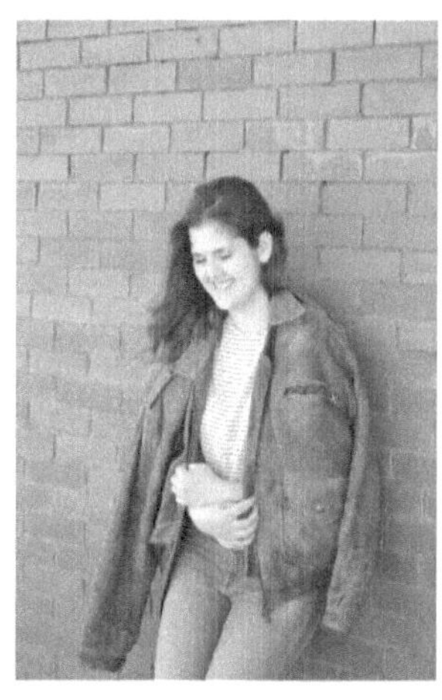

Dree Christiano is zealous for old movies, and old music. Always ready for exciting adventures, her heart is happiest with her computer on her lap or with a book in her hands. The lives she wishes to live herself, she lives in her books. Her extreme hobby is writing. She immerses herself in as much World War II history as she can, and enjoys learning fun facts about the era. Two of her favorite movies are *Mrs. Miniver* (1942), and *His Girl Friday* (1940). Dree and her mother make their home in a little white house on the edge of a small farm community, Hope, Kansas.

"Whatever your hand findeth to do,
do it with all your might."
Ecclesiastes 9:10

www.ingramcontent.com/pod-product-compliance
Lightning Source LLC
Chambersburg PA
CBHW031322060726
47590CB00003B/1303